Victoria's Busy Day

From the series *Victoria's Torton Tales*

Written by
Wendy Wakelin

Illustrations by
Viv Harries

www.victoriastortontales.com
Copyright © 2016 Wendy Wakelin
All rights reserved.
ISBN: 1519569238
ISBN-13: 978-1519569233

Victoria was a shiny green traction engine, with two large back wheels and two smaller wheels at the front. She had three brass bands around her boiler and a tall, elegant, black chimney with a gleaming brass top.

She lived with Mr. Seward and his other traction engines in the small town of Torton.

Mr. Seward and his engineer, George, would steam her from farm to farm helping with the harvest. When the harvest was finished, Victoria would pull wagons stacked high with all sorts of things, from bricks, gravel, soil and tar, to even furniture, making deliveries all over the place.

Victoria was a very hard working engine and enjoyed having fun too. While puffing through the villages and towns, she would see how many people would jump when she gave a quick "Peep, peep!" on her whistle.

Every morning at 6 o'clock, Mr. Seward and George would come down to the yard and open the large wooden doors on the front of the workshop.

On fine, sunny mornings, the sunlight would stream in and gently warm Victoria's face. Mr. Seward and George would light her fire, build up steam, oil her joints and then set off together to do the day's work.

One morning, Mr. Seward came into the workshop and said, "Good morning Victoria. Today we're going up to Mr. Andrews' farm with a trailer to help bring the grain in from the fields." This made Victoria excited, as it meant she would get to see another of Mr. Seward's engines, Albert.

"Oh good!" Victoria thought as they set off, "Albert has been away for several days now. It'll be lovely to see him."

The sun was shining, the birds were singing and Victoria was very happy.

When they reached Mr. Andrews' farm she could see Albert standing by the threshing machine in the lower wheat field.

Albert was a strong little engine. He stood a little bit shorter than Victoria, with his back wheels being slightly smaller than hers. He was a cheeky engine too.

"Mornin' Tor. Good to see ya!" Albert called across the field.

"Good morning, Albert," Victoria replied, "it's such a lovely day."

Albert smiled and gave a "Toot, tooooot!" on his whistle as his driver opened the regulator.

Albert's flywheel started turning. Around the flywheel was a large belt which ran to the threshing machine. As his flywheel gathered speed the threshing machine whirred into life.

Victoria made her way across the field to the back of the whirring threshing machine where sacks were being filled with grain and men loaded them into her trailer.

Everyone worked hard and soon the trailer was full.

"Peep, peep! I'm off now," Victoria called to Albert, "I'll be back for more, later" and she puffed off up the track.

The grain had to be taken to the farmyard at the top of the hill. It was a long climb.

"Come on! Pull, pull! Come on! Pull, pull!" she puffed, "I will get to the top." Eventually she cleared the top of the hill and could see the farmyard just ahead.

"Hurray!" Victoria cheered, "I've made it!"

Victoria pulled into the farmyard through the gate and round to where the grain was to be stored.

While the farm workers unloaded the trailer, Mr. Seward gave her a nice cool drink of water. Victoria enjoyed the short rest in the sun.

"That's better," she whispered to herself, "especially after that long climb."

Before long it was time to head back down to the field.

Albert was still working hard. "Back again?" he said.

"Yes, I'm ready for my next load," replied Victoria.

It was hard work pulling a trailer full of grain up the hill, but Victoria didn't mind. She was out in the warm sunshine and with her friend Albert.

The men filled the trailer, and Victoria puffed up the hill again and again, until it was lunchtime. Albert could rest now, and the two engines dozed off.

All too soon, it was time to get back to work.

"Wake up," called Mr. Seward with a smile, "time for work again."

The trailer was loaded with the heavy sacks of grain and Victoria headed up the hill to the farmyard again.

While waiting for the men to unload the trailer she noticed something in the corner of the barn, something yellowish caught the afternoon sunlight. It was the brass chimney top of a little traction engine.

He was covered in dust and looked like he hadn't been used for quite some time.

"Hello," said Victoria, "who are you?"

"Who, me?" replied the little engine, "I'm called Pop."

"My name's Victoria. Why aren't you out here helping with the harvest?"

"I'd love to be out there in the sunshine, but my safety valve doesn't work properly," said Pop, "and Mr. Andrews can't afford to mend me", with that a tear rolled down his cheek.

"Don't be sad," said Victoria "Mr. Seward can mend engines," she added, trying to cheer-up the little engine. "I'll ask him to come and see if he can help you."

"Oh, thank you!" said Pop, looking a little happier.

Before heading back down to the field Victoria asked Mr. Seward if he would help Pop.

"I don't see why not," he said, "but, it'll have to wait until we've finished getting the grain in."

"Thank you," said Victoria with a smile on her face, "he will be pleased."

Victoria told Pop that Mr. Seward would come and see him once the harvest was finished.

When Victoria got back to the workshop that evening, she told Albert all about Pop and how Mr. Seward said he would try to help him.

It had been a very busy day and she soon fell asleep, wondering when Pop would be fixed.

How a Steam Engine Works

Locomotive Type Boiler

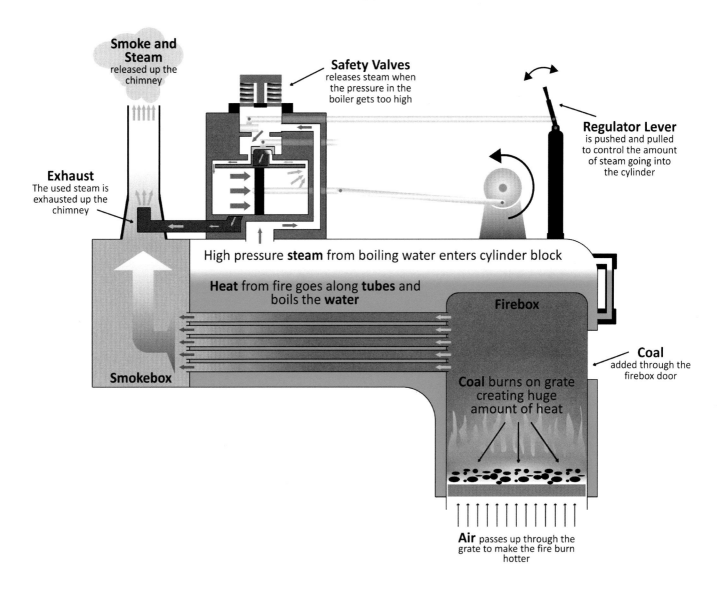

Smoke and Steam released up the chimney

Safety Valves releases steam when the pressure in the boiler gets too high

Regulator Lever is pushed and pulled to control the amount of steam going into the cylinder

Exhaust The used steam is exhausted up the chimney

High pressure **steam** from boiling water enters cylinder block

Heat from fire goes along **tubes** and boils the **water**

Firebox

Coal added through the firebox door

Smokebox

Coal burns on grate creating huge amount of heat

Air passes up through the grate to make the fire burn hotter

All steam engines have a boiler. The boiler holds a lot of water, a bit like a giant kettle. A fire is used to heat up the water in the boiler to make it boil. When water boils it turns to steam. As more steam is made from the boiling water the pressure in the boiler increases.

Victoria is a Traction Engine. Like most of her steam engine friends, she has a locomotive type boiler, similar to a railway engine. Victoria's boiler holds 150 gallons / 680 litres of water.

Once the water is boiling the steam collects at the top of the boiler and goes up into the cylinder block. When the regulator lever is pushed and pulled it controls the amount of steam that's let through into the cylinder. The steam then pushes the piston.

After the steam has pushed the piston, it's released along an exhaust pipe and up the chimney. As it rushes up the chimney it pulls the hot air and smoke from the fire along the tubes through the boiler, heating up the water and making more steam.

The pushing of the piston backwards and forwards turns a crankshaft. On the end of the crankshaft is a flywheel. The flywheel helps the crankshaft keep turning and can be used to drive other machinery by running a belt around it and across to a wheel on another machine. This is how Albert drives the Threshing Machine in the story of "Victoria's Busy Day".

Also on the crankshaft there are gears which can be engaged and used to turn the back wheels on a Traction Engine. This is how Victoria and her friends are able to drive along on the road.

Remember to look out for...

Pop Comes to Sewards' Yard

The second story in the series *Victoria's Torton Tales.* It had been quite some time since poor old Pop was last in steam and helping Mr Andrews on his farm. When Pop was found by Victoria and Mr. Seward they said they would help him, but that was weeks ago! Pop longed to be out in the sunshine instead of being stuck in a cold, damp and dusty barn with junk piled up around him...

Made in the USA
Middletown, DE
14 February 2019